CHRISTMAS IN THE MULTIVERSE

A MULTIVERSE INVESTIGATIONS STORY

R E MCLEAN

JOIN THE TEAM

If you enjoy this book, you can join the Multiverse Investigators team to get new stories as they're published for FREE.

Please see the end of this book for full details.

Thanks,
RE McLean

ONE

HO HO HO

IT WAS the day before Christmas Eve, and for the love of Santa and all his evil minions, Alex Strand didn't want to be working.

But here she was at the San Francisco morgue, having received an urgent call from her boss twenty minutes earlier.

She pushed through the double doors and spotted Monique leaning against a wall, muttering into her phone. She was a tall, willowy woman who exuded sophistication until she opened her mouth. Her voice was like the loudest and most obnoxious punk band you could imagine—on a day when they'd been munching on barbed wire.

"Where's Mike?" asked Alex.

"At the MIU. Getting ready."

Sergeant Mike Long, Alex's partner, was probably trying to tame his facial hair. Last time she'd seen him, his beard was in the shape of an Adelie Penguin.

"I don't see why you need us for Santa getting shot."

As the Multiverse Investigations Unit's resident physicist, Alex was normally only summoned to crime scenes with a trace of the inter-dimensional about them. A straightforward shooting wasn't her concern, even if it was the Macy's Santa, the pinnacle of Santadom for all the city's impersonators of the red-suited man.

Monique waggled a finger at Alex. She muttered something that sounded a lot like *pasta and meatballs* into her phone then hung up.

"Follow me."

They passed from one patch of quivering fluorescent light to the next, stopping at a door that was suitably imposing and cold, like the doorway to the pits of doom. Monique pushed it open and called out.

"Doctor Sanchez, it's Lieutenant Williams. I have my colleague."

A short woman wearing a lab coat at least three sizes too big appeared from the shadows. She wore a heavy bloodstained apron.

"Hello," the woman said, extending a gloved hand. Alex shook the fingertips.

"Hello, I'm Alex Strand. I work with Lieutenant Williams."

"She's told me all about you." The pathologist shrugged her shoulders. "Short, ginger Scotswoman with an inferiority complex."

Alex frowned. "I wouldn't be quite so—"

"Don't worry, *lassie*. That's not what she said. Just my intuition."

So this was what a doctor with the bedside manner of a mass murderer did for a job. At least the dead wouldn't hear her making assumptions about them.

The pathologist turned away. "He's over here. I'm not sure what to do with him."

They followed her to a spotlit gurney. On it was an elderly man with a large stomach, pale skin and bushy white beard. He looked to be at least six and a half feet tall.

Alex wrinkled her nose. "Where's the wound?"

The pathologist shook her head. "That's just it. It's gone."

"Gone?"

"Vanished. The first time he woke up."

Alex looked at Monique. "You thought you'd wind me up to celebrate the holidays."

Monique shook her head. "Wait. Watch him."

Alex squared her shoulders, aware of the pathologist's skin-piercing gaze. She probably had Alex's bra size in her head and knew that she was wearing days-of-the-week underpants. Today was a Tuesday, and she was wearing Saturday. No harm in optimism.

They watched the body in silence. His skin was smooth, despite the white hair, and there was a hint of ruddiness to his cheeks.

Alex blinked.

She stepped back.

She looked at Monique, who nodded.

"Is this normal?" she whispered.

"Nope," replied Dr Sanchez. "No more normal than Saturday coming on a Tuesday." She winked at Alex.

Alex looked back at the body. His cheeks were definitely getting redder. In fact they now looked as ruddy as a drunk's nose. Alex could hear Monique's breathing, as loud and hoarse as her voice.

Then he twitched.

Not a big twitch. Not the kind of twitch you'd make if you were about to sneeze, but more the reaction to a mosquito flying exactly three inches away from your face.

Alex held her breath.

He did it again. It was a bigger twitch this time, as if

the mosquito had come in to land. Alex batted the air. Maybe it was his reflexes. He'd fart next.

Then he opened his eyes.

Alex shrieked and jumped back. She slammed into Monique who pushed a hand into her back.

The pathologist barked a laugh. "Got me the first time too."

"The first time?"

"He's been doing it on and off for the last hour."

The body sat up. He widened his mouth into a smile.

"Ho ho ho," he said.

"Watch," said the pathologist.

Santa fell back to the gurney. His cheeks paled and his body went slack. Dr Sanchez placed a hand on his wrist.

"He's dead."

Monique whispered into Alex's ear. "One for the MIU, don't you think?"

TWO

HEISENBERG

THEY STOOD outside the elevator down to the MIU, in the basement of the Hall of Justice. Monique hadn't taken her eyes off Alex the whole journey from the morgue.

"You sure you're OK?" she asked.

Alex nodded. Her pulse was like that of a hamster and she was sweating. But she wasn't about to let Monique know that.

"Whatever this is," Monique said, "It's not from our world. Fluxing in and out of life like that."

"Right."

Monique put a hand on Alex's arm. "First visit to the morgue isn't easy."

"It's not that." Alex had seen a dead body before; her own mum, three years ago. She was attempting to track her down in parallel universes so they could be reunited.

"There's no physical phenomenon that involves fluxing in and out of life and death," she said. "Not when you're being watched, anyway."

"What about Shroedinger's cat?"

Alex frowned. "How did you know?"

"You work for a top secret police unit, kid. Of course we know about your weird cat."

Alex's cat, Shroedinger, was a quantum cat. He had a habit of dying in his box. It was very inconvenient, especially when her best friend Rik popped by with his cat-loving daughters.

"Shroedinger can only change his quantum state when no one's observing him. The Heisenberg Uncertainty Principle states that—"

Monique held up a hand. "Save it, boffin."

"But that Santa. We saw him die. That can't happen."

"It just did."

"You sure he doesn't have some kind of condition? Narcolepsy, or something?"

"He was shot, Alex. Right in the chest. I saw it, at the crime scene. Christmas at Macy's has never been so frantic."

"So what do you think?"

"No idea. But Madge has an idea."

Madge was a member of the MIU team, who masterminded communications between Alex's world and others.

"Don't you have his address? Any next of kin?" Alex imagined being told that your husband or father had been gunned down two days before Christmas, dressed as Santa. Then she thought of her dad. He'd found a job as Santa in their local Poundland, back home in Scotland. *Don't be daft*, she told herself. Gun crime, in Gretna?

"He's not from around here. He's from a place called San TaClaus."

"Very apt."

"Seriously. It's the universe where Christmas comes from."

"Christmas doesn't come from anywhere. It developed from centuries of pagan tradition."

"Uh-uh. It comes from San TaClaus. And I'm sending you and Mike there."

"Of course you are."

Alex hoped this mission could be over quickly. She hit the elevator button. As she stepped inside, Monique held the door.

"One more thing. Alex. This guy is important."

"Why? Who is he?"

"He's the real thing. Santa. Saint Nick. Father Christmas. The original and best."

"Don't be daft."

"Uh-huh. You have to get him back where he belongs. Or there'll be no Christmas."

THREE

ELF

THE MIU WAS DECORATED for the holidays in its own eccentric style. Garlands of mistletoe were draped over posters of Einstein wearing a Christmas jumper, topped by baubles that looked a lot like atomic models.

On all the surfaces were models of a molecule consisting of Oxygen, Hydrogen and Nitrogen atoms.

Alex picked one up. "What's this?"

"It's called Red Nose," replied Nemesis. "By-product of Rudolphomycin."

"Just ignore him, my dear," said Madge. "He gets very excited at this time of year."

Alex put it down and headed for the double doors that led to Sarita's base of operations. Sarita was the unit's material scientist, and she occupied a constantly shifting white space with Escher-like dimensions.

Mike was already there, Sarita admiring the costume she had given him.

Mike's eyes were flashing and his eyebrows knitted together, and not just because his last jump had turned them into something resembling a yeti's left ear.

"You look very—er—very festive," Alex said.

"Shut up."

Sarita gave him a playful slap on the shoulder. It was covered in brown, spotted fur. Or a simulacrum of fur, at least.

"You look the part," said Sarita. "That's the point."

Sarita had a habit of seeing them off to alternate realities dressed in the least appropriate clothes possible. In Silicon City they'd arrived in garishly colored outfits and quickly been given darker, less obtrusive clothing by Madonna, the genius who'd invented the Hive and presided over Silicon City's version of the MIU, the Multiverse Operations Organization. Or MOO, for short. For their jump to Greater Castro, Sarita had produced two outfits worthy of the winning floats at San Francisco Pride. The only problem was that in a world where being gay is the norm, wearing pink feather boas and a chest wig made them the local equivalent of Amish.

So Alex was more than a little worried about Mike's reindeer costume. It looked like it had been stolen from an elementary school staging San Francisco's most poorly funded Christmas production.

"Why so scruffy?" asked Alex. "Your outfits are normally perfectly tailored."

Sarita tipped her nose. "Intel, sweetie. Intel."

Alex blushed at the *sweetie*. She was trying to hide the massive crush she had on Sarita, and failing badly.

"So what will I be wearing?"

A rack of headgear swooshed towards then and Sarita grabbed a pair of fluffy antlers. She plonked them on Mike's head.

Sarita stood back to admire her handiwork. "Perfect." She clapped her hands and turned to Alex. "Now you."

Alex hoped she wasn't going to be playing the back end of the reindeer.

"Now." Sarita drummed her fingers against her perfectly smooth chin. "You're short, pale and ginger. What shall I dress you as?"

"I think—" said Mike. Alex glared at him.

"I've got it!" exclaimed Sarita. "An elf."

Alex sighed. It didn't matter. Madonna would find them new outfits as soon as they arrived in Hive Earth, their stopping-off point for all jumps.

Sarita opened a white drawer, perfectly camouflaged in the bright space, and pulled out an elf outfit.

"Go and put this on. Then come back and get your gadgets."

M oments later, Alex emerged from the changing room in her elf outfit. Stripy blue and white tights, a long red jacket with gold buttons, shoes so long they tripped her over with every step. And a tiny yellow hat that perched on top of her ginger curls.

She looked like a ten-year-old.

Mike nodded. "Very fetching."

"At least I don't look like I've been dragged through a hedge by Donner and Blitzen."

"Oh!" said Sarita. "That reminds me."

She reached into the pocket of her jade leather jacket and pulled out a red nose. She popped it onto Mike's nose.

She turned to Alex. "I've got two, if you want one."

"No thanks. Not very elf-like."

"Suit yourself. Now. You need some special kit for this jump. Take these."

She plunged a hand into her inside pocket and brought out a beautifully wrapped parcel and a candy cane.

"That's your bitbox," she said, gesturing at the parcel. A bitbox was a communications device developed in Hive Earth.

Mike shoved the bitbox into his reindeer leg. Alex sniffed the candy cane.

"Don't eat it," said Sarita. "Not yet."

"Why not?"

"You'll find out. Now, time to jump."

FOUR
RUDOPLH

NEMESIS AND MADGE were waiting for them. Madge wore a red cardigan with a reindeer design and Nemesis had made himself look festive by dyeing his normally white shock of hair bright red.

"I like the hair," said Alex.

He put a hand to it. "What? What's happened to it?"

"Sorry," said Alex. "It looks fine. No change."

"Hello, dears," sad Madge. A pair of glasses on a wire entwined with tinsel floated over her ample bosom and the reindeer on her knitwear seemed to catch the light and dance the can-can as Alex watched. She blinked and they switched to going a conga.

"Hey Madge," said Alex. "Ready for us?"

"Yes, my dear. And we've got a treat for you today."

Alex narrowed her eyes. Madge's treats normally involved saltwater taffy.

"A direct jump," Madge continued.

Nemesis was at the circular console in the centre of the vast wood-lined space that formed the heart of the MIU. He jabbed at the screen in front of him.

"We're sending you straight to San TaClaus," he said. "No stop-off in Hive Earth."

Alex felt herself deflate. No Silicon City meant no outfit change.

"Isn't it safer to go via the MOO?"

"We don't have time, my dear," said Madge. "The Macy's Santa isn't the only one."

"Not the only one?" asked Mike. "Surely there's only one genuine Santa?"

"Of course. No, he's not the only one missing."

"What?" said Alex. Her chest felt tight.

"Santas all over the world are disappearing into thin air. We've had reports of twelve more in San Francisco. Forty-two in LA, although I'm sure that's just their idea of a cosmic joke. Two thousand and seventy three across the States. And," she looked at Alex, "three hundred and seventy one and a half in Scotland."

Alex swallowed. "My dad?"

Madge shook her head. "We don't have any IDs as yet. But all the big stores have been affected. All the amusement parks, and libraries."

"Poundland isn't a major store," replied Alex. "Maybe he'll be OK."

Madge cocked her head. "I hope so. But let's send you over there to make sure, eh?"

Alex followed Mike to the Spinner. She tried not to think of her dad, scowling at the kids on his knee and refusing to tell them Santa would bring them a PlayStation. He meant well really.

She heard shuffling, followed by what could only be braying.

"What's that?"

Nemesis grinned. "That's Rudolph."

"Don't talk about Mike like that," returned Alex.

"Seriously," replied Nemesis, as a fully grown, fur-covered reindeer wearing green tinsel in his antlers appeared in the doorway to the Spinner. "He's going to get you to San TaClaus. Stick a reindeer in the Spinner and you end up in San TaClaus. Trust the technology."

Alex eyed Rudolph. His nose was flashing like a stripper at a hen party. "Doesn't look very technological to me."

"That's the beauty of it," said Nemesis, ignoring Madge's sigh. "It's a quantum nose."

Alex opened her mouth to ask a question then thought better of it. If that was a quantum nose, she was a chipmunk in stripy tights.

Mike grabbed her arm. "Come on."

They stepped inside the Spinner. It was glowing red, with green patches swirling around the walls. Tinsel draped from the ceiling and in one corner was a fake Christmas tree decorated in shades of orange and purple.

"Like it?" asked Madge.

"Errr…"

"Me neither. But the reindeer does and that's what counts. Time to go, my dears."

The door swished shut. The reindeer approached the tree and begin to nibble at its branches. Before Alex could tell it to stop, the world disappeared in a blur of tinsel, fairy lights and baubles.

FIVE
GALLOP

ALEX STUMBLED out of the Spinner. Her stomach was making noises that made her think she had a performing seal in there, and she could feel beads of sweat popping out on her face.

She leaned over and retched, spattering the ground with her lunch. Fortunately she'd been sticking to her white food diet and the flecks of cauliflower were almost camouflaged by the snow.

Mike was behind her. His face was green and he'd grown a—

"Of course!" she laughed, nausea leaving her.

Mike frowned at her and put a hand to his chin. The Spinner always had the same effect on Mike, one that irritated him more than a mosquito in a nunnery and which he refused to acknowledge.

Alex bit her lip. Mike was waving his fingers in and out of his beard. It was full, and thick, and bushy.

"Go on then," he said. "What color is it?"

"White. Can I have a present please?"

"Don't."

He pushed past her and stepped out into the snow. It was clean, virgin snow, the sort of snow you wake up to when school is cancelled, your toboggan is ready to go and all is perfect with the world. Flakes of it danced around them, twirling in the air like something out of a movie.

Alex stuck out her tongue, waiting for the crisp freshness to hit.

"Urrgh!" she spluttered, spitting it out.

"What?" Mike asked.

"Try one."

He stuck his tongue out. It protruded from his beard like the tiny tongue of a cat, or maybe a white-maned lion. The snowflakes got nowhere near it.

He held his hand out to catch some flakes.

"Wait," he said. "Why is it so warm?"

"It's paper."

"Paper."

"Fake snow."

She dropped to the ground and lay in it, windmilling her limbs to make snow angels. Paper angels. She sprang up again.

"So--what else is fake?"

They looked around. Rudolph had emerged from the Spinner and was happily grazing on the paper that coated the ground around them. Alex poked him.

"Are you real, boy?"

He raised his head to glare at her. His tinselly antlers were covered in flakes of pristine white paper. They were huge, as big as gobstoppers.

"Sorry," she muttered. The deer turned to saunter up the hill ahead of them, pausing from time to time to eat.

"How will we get back, if he disappears?"

"Don't worry," replied Mike. "Madge has it covered. I'll contact her on the bitbox when we need to get home."

He reached into the pocket of his red jacket and brought out the bitbox. It was perfectly wrapped with a perky looking green ribbon on top.

"Nice," she said.

Mike shuffled out of the reindeer suit. Underneath, he was earring jeans and a Christmas sweater. It sported a row of elves doing the Macarena.

"Madge?" asked Alex.

"Early Christmas present." He slid the bitbox into a pocket that had been knitted into the front of his sweater. The elves shuffled along and mooned at them.

They were in a forest clearing, with tall conifers surrounding them. To the South West was a steep slope upwards, fringed by nibbled trees. Rudolph was a hundred yards ahead, making his way up the hill.

"Madge said to go to the top of Mount Davidson," said Mike. "Which is that way."

"Right."

They started trudging upwards through the snow. Alex adopted the stride she normally used on snowy mountains back home in Scotland, but soon realized that wading through paper was quite different from snow. Instead of crunching nicely under her tread, the paper squished and swooshed, forming swirls and eddies around her. After a few steps she had a pile of flakes banked up against her shins, slowing her progress.

She stopped to shake them off. She felt hot in her elf suit, and dreaded the reaction of anyone they might meet here. This place was probably a movie set, populated by actors and producers in clothes more suited to the temperature. So much for blending in.

She altered her tread, picking her feet up and placing them down squarely with each stride. After twenty strides she was worn out.

"This is daft," she said. "There has to be a better way."

Rudolph had stopped and was chewing at a tree.

Mike paused to stretch, his fists balled in the small of his back. He flung his reindeer antlers off and threw them to the ground. He coughed, then almost choked on a white hair that had strayed into his mouth.

"Why don't we try riding him?" Alex said.

"What?"

Alex approached the deer.

"Here, boy," she muttered, holding a hand out. "Minou minou."

The reindeer looked up as abruptly as if she'd yanked on a chain around his neck. She smiled, thinking of Shroedinger; this was a surefire way of getting his attention.

"Minou minou."

The reindeer dropped the branch he was chewing and approached her. She held her breath.

"What the hell?" said Mike.

"He's a quantum deer. He likes French."

"What?"

"Quantum cats like French, it seems quantum reindeer do too."

The reindeer dipped his head as he reached her. He lowered onto his front legs, inviting her to climb up.

"Ha!" she cried. "This is all my Christmases rolled into one."

"Don't be too hasty," said Mike. "We still have to work out where Santa has got to."

"Maybe Rudolph will lead the way. He seems like a clever chap. Don't you, boy?"

She was on Rudolph's back now, clinging to his fur. "Come on," she told Mike. "Get up."

Rudolph dipped his rear legs as obligingly as the

world's most obsequious butler. Mike grabbed Alex's arm and climbed up. At last he was behind her, gripping her waist.

"Not too tight," she said.

"Don't worry. I know about you and Sarita."

Alex felt her face turn so purple it was now probably The Face Formerly Known As Alex's.

"Don't know what you're talking about,"she replied, thinking of the kiss she'd grabbed after she and Sarita had jumped together for the first time. The arguments they'd shared, and the secrets Sarita was keeping.

"Don't worry," he replied, miming zipping his lip. She shook her head and dug her heels into Rudolph's flank.

"Giddy up!"

She braced herself for the jolt of Rudolph breaking into a run, if reindeer did run. Canter? Gallop? Or did they have a vocabulary of their own?

Rudolph didn't budge.

"Mush," she said.

Nothing.

"Run!" shouted Mike. Rudolph made a noise that sounded like a snort of derision.

Alex thought for a moment.

"Hang on," she muttered.

"What?" asked Mike. "This was a daft idea. Let's get down."

She raised a hand to silence him. "No." She paused.

"Allons-y!" she cried.

The reindeer sprang into life.

SIX

CANDY

RUDOLF WAS SURPRISINGLY SPRIGHTLY, for such a heavy creature. Within minutes they were at the top of Mount Davidson.

Alex and Mike slid down from the reindeer's back. Mike was out of breath and wheezing.

"You OK?" asked Alex.

He nodded, then coughed. "I'll be fine. Seem to have gained a few pounds on the jump."

It wasn't just MIke's beard that had changed on this jump. His middle was distinctly broader and his skin ruddier. The elves had disappeared from his sweater and it had turned red. He looked a lot like—

"Don't say anything," he said. "I'm not Santa."

"No."

She hoped her dad didn't look as ridiculous as this, in the outfit the pound store would have given him. But Mike's beard was real. His sweater was now made of a plush red velvet that made him stand out like a pool of blood against the snow. Dad's beard would be fake, and his suit made of polyester. And he would probably insist on wearing the tartan Santa hat he wore for Christmas every year. Santa was a Scot, he claimed. It explained all the whisky he drank.

Rudolph plodded away and started nibbling on another tree. Beyond him, a view of the city panned out below them.

This wasn't the San Francisco she knew. It looked more like something from a chocolate box. Wooden cabins with snow-topped roofs fanned out from long, brightly lit streets festooned with Christmas lights and decorations.

At the edge of it all was a pale blue Bay, shimmering in the low sunshine. The Golden Gate Bridge was right where it should be, but instead of being shrouded in mist, it looked like it had been sprayed with icing sugar.

"This must be the place," said Mike.

Behind him was another cabin. Instead of logs, it was made from oversized Tootsie Rolls. The windows were brightly colored and opaque, like the windows in the gingerbread houses they sold at Macy's.

She trudged though the paper snow and ran a finger down a window. It felt sticky and warm.

She licked her finger.

"Mmm."

Mike followed her lead. He licked his finger then reached for the window again. "Jolly Ranchers"

"Best one I've ever tasted."

"Do you think we can eat the walls?"

She shrugged. "Not if we don't want the building to collapse."

"We should stop. We've got a job to do."

"I know," she said, taking another lick. "But this is so good."

She pawed at the windows, scoping her fingers along them as fast as she could, This stuff didn't just taste good; it made her feel good, too. Warmth was swelling in her stomach, along with a feeling of well-being.

She leaned in towards a window, wondering if she could get away with licking the panes. Through the distorted candy, she spotted movement.

She raised a hand. "Stop."

Mike was tugging at his beard, trying to tease out sticky clumps. For once, he wasn't grumbling. "What?"

"There's someone in there," she whispered.

He leaned in next to her, putting a hand up against the window. She pulled him back.

"We need to get in there," she said. "This is where Madge told us to come. Center of the disturbances."

"Can't we eat a bit more first?"

His cheeks were flushed and his mouth smeared with gluey stickiness. HIs pupils had dilated so much he looked like a My Little Pony.

"No," she said. "It's drugged."

"It's candy. That's all."

"Look at my eyes. Are my pupils dilated?"

She realized that the world had become brighter, as if someone had shone a spotlight on their surroundings.

He leaned in. "Yeah. Christ, Alex, your eyes look like they could swallow a reindeer whole."

She took a deep breath, and spat at the ground.

"Don't eat any more."

He wiped his fingers on his suit. "No."

They looked through the window again. Alex could hear voices. There was a center of light, blurred through the candy pane, and shapes moving around in front of it.

She squinted and put her face closer to the pane, making sure she didn't touch it.

"What can you see?" asked Mike.

"Dunno. I think there's people in there."

A face appeared on the other side of the window. Alex gasped and fell backwards. Mike stumbled with her, the two of them tumbling into the paper snow.

"Run," she hissed. "We've been spotted."

SEVEN

COMRADES

THEY RAN along the front of the building and hurled themselves around a wall to its side. Behind them, Alex heard a door open.

"Hello?"

The voice was high-pitched, like its owner had been inhaling helium. "Who's out there?"

They ran again, more slowly this time, careful not to make a sound. Alex was glad of the paper flakes to deaden their footsteps.

Behind the cabin was a barn. A large, open-fronted structure, made not of Twinkies but of Snickers bars.

Mike gestured towards it. He was crouched on the ground, his back against the wall of the cabin. He had his hands in front of his chest and his fingers steepled as if they were a gun.

"What're you doing?" Alex whispered.

He looked down at his hands then swiftly brought them to his sides. "Sorry. Habit."

She wondered in how many universes he'd been able to get his hands on a weapon. The only object they'd ever carried through the Spinner had been the bitbox, and its only weapon was the high-pitched wailing it made when Alex tried to break into it.

Mike started to run to the barn. Alex followed. It had a high door made of red wood. It gleamed as if freshly painted, and sparkled as the light hit it.

They yanked it open, tumbled inside and leaned against it.

In front of them was the largest, most ornate sleigh Alex had ever seen. It gleamed like a pin so new it was just a twinkle in its mother's eye. Its runners were made of gold encrusted with sparkling diamonds and its sides were fashioned from a heavy wood painted the same gleaming red as the barn doors. On top was a glass roof that glinted in the low light.

"I'll check if there's anyone in this thing," said Mike. "You watch the cabin."

Alex eased the high door open and peered out. She could hear two voices.

"What did you see, Gerald?"

"A face. Licking the window."

"You've been drinking to much mead."

"No, sir. Don't touch the stuff."

"Hmm. Anyway, there's no one out here. Maybe you need to have a lie down."

"But sir—"

"No buts, Corporal. Let's get back inside. Horace hasn't finished speaking yet."

Alex opened the door further. Between them and the house were two people. They were both no more than four feet tall. One was blushing so hard he might turn into a plum at any moment. The other frowned at him. Instead of wearing military uniform, as she's expected, they were dressed like she was. One wore a red suit, the other green.

Both had pointy hats with bells on the end, and shoots so long they'd make it difficult to walk.

"Sleigh's clear. Military?" asked Mike.

"Sort of."

He looked over her head.

"Military elves," she said. "That's a new one."

The two elves went to a door in the rear of the cabin that seemed to be made from a giant Hershey bar. The one in red, the frowning one, opened it and ushered the other through. HIs colleague ducked as he did so, leaning away from the other elf as if afraid of being struck.

"Let's follow them," Mike said.

The door closed behind the elves. Alex and Mike crept towards it, keeping low. There were no windows in this side of the building, just a solid wall of Twinkies.

They stopped at the door. Alex put a hand on it. It was cool to the touch. She resisted the urge to bite it.

She looked at Mike. His beard had matted where the candy had stuck and he looked like Santa after too many whiskies. His pupils had returned to normal and his face registered quiet determination.

They waited for a few minutes, then Mike turned the doorknob. It squeaked faintly and he stopped, his gaze on Alex. She could feel her heart beating.

Mike wrinkled his nose. His thick white mustache was straying into his nostrils. He started to shudder. He stared at Alex, wide-eyed, his hand not moving from the doorknob.

He started to twitch, his nose twisting itself into contorted shapes. He took a stilted breath.

Alex grabbed the elf hat from her head and shoved it under his nose. Silently, Mike sneezed into it.

"Thanks."

She shrugged. He wiped his nose on the hat and handed it back to her.

She grimaced. "Keep it," she whispered.

He shoved it inside his suit, sniffing. He patted his mustache to smooth it away from his nostrils.

He turned the doorknob further and eased the door open just a crack.

Alex peered through. She could see a wall of small backs. There were elves in there. Lots of them.

Mike opened the door further. There was a voice, high-pitched like the two Alex had heard outside. Someone was making a speech.

"Comrades," the elf cried. "It is time for us to prevail. For too long we have been expected to slave away all year, making toys, filling stockings with candy, hacking into Amazon wishlists. It's our turn to have a Merry Christmas!"

Muttering ran though the crowd of elves. There was a mood of agitation in the room, of nerves being frayed to breaking point.

"We have the ur-Santa in custody," the voice continued. "This gives us bargaining power, comrades. Brother Geoff and I have spent the last three hundred and sixty two Boxing Days in negotiation with the Council of Santas. You know as well, as I do, brothers and sisters, that this has been fruitless. Arbitration has not worked. The Santas are refusing to bend. Now is the time for us to act, to claim what we are due!"

The elves jumped up and down, applauding. Two at the back tossed their pointy hats in the air, then fell to the floor, scrabbling for them under the feet of their colleagues.

"Isn't it a bit, er, a bit... extreme?" Another voice, even higher-pitched, and shaking.

"Extreme, Comrade Rodney? Extreme?" The first voice asked. Alex could imagine its owner scanning the crowd, checking for dissent, emphasizing the drama of his rhetoric. "I'll tell you what I call extreme. Working for three hundred and sixty three days a year with no pay, that's extreme. Being forced to sleep in shifts with the reindeer, that's extreme. Toilet breaks only when there's an R in the month, that's extreme!"

The elves applauded again.

"Too right, Brother Horace," came another voice. "By September my bladder is so full I could fill the Bay with its contents!"

The elves laughed. Then there was a hush. Alex could imagine the speechmaker—Horace—putting his hand up for silence. She'd met men like this before. Union officials at her dad's old workplace, the shoelace factory. Little men with a modicum of power who liked to puff themselves up.

Expect this one was littler than most. And he had Santa.

"We need to get in there," she whispered. "Look for Santa, while they're distracted."

Mike nodded. He pushed the door open a few more inches.

Alex scanned the room. To one side was a doorway. It was festooned with sparkly red tape, with the words PRISON DO NOT ENTER stamped on it.

"Seriously? They've made it that obvious?"

"It could be a bluff," replied Mike.

"Gotta be worth a go."

"Comrades, let me share our plan!" shouted Horace. "Tomorrow is Christmas Eve. Children across the Multiverse will be expecting a visit from their version of Santa. Saint Nick on Old Earth. Silicon Santa in Hive Earth. The

Wisp in Fogtown. Pere Noel in Le Monde Francais, or as I like to call it, Ribbitworld."

The elves laughed politely at the terrible joke.

"Come on," hissed Mike. "Stay low."

They pushed the door open, slowly. They started to crawl towards the taped-off door. They kept to the walls, glancing upwards at the elves' backs to check they hadn't been seen.

Mike was in front of Alex. His jeans had morphed into red velvet trousers and his ample rump blocked her field of vision. He stopped, making her almost crash into him. He was shuddering.

"You OK?" she whispered.

He turned to her, his eyes wide with dread. His nose was twitching.

He was about to sneeze.

She pointed at her head, then at his suit. He widened his eyes further in recognition and plunged his hand into his suit, pulling out the hat. He clasped it to his nose.

He gulped, wiping his nose with Alex's elf hat. She was never wearing that thing again.

The bell at the tip of the hat shook. Alex stared at it, her mouth dropping open. She reached out to grab it.

The bell jingled.

Her hand closed on it. Too late.

An elf next to her turned. He looked down. More elves followed. They whispered to each other. Alex could feel the floor vibrate as the crowd turned to see.

Then there was a cry. In a high, squeaky voice, but a very loud one.

"Santa!"

EIGHT
IMPOSTOR

THE ELVES FELL ON MIKE, yelling in their high-pitched voices. The bells on their hats and feet jingled as they flew at him, and they screamed like a gang of street cats fighting over a fishbone.

Alex waited for them to grab her, to pull her away and expose her for a fake. But they didn't.

She realized that down here, on the floor, they couldn't tell that she was a foot taller than them.

She decided to stay put.

Almost a hundred bodies were piled onto Mike now, forming a toppling, writhing mass of green fabric, bells and twisted faces. The elves dressed in red hung back, goading the others. Their eyes danced with excitement.

At last every green-clad elf had hurled him- or herself into the pile.

The pile shifted. It started to grow, as if being pushed at from within.

It quivered, then shook, then teetered, then it came crashing down, elves scattering everywhere.

They groaned and cried, gabbing at limbs, heads,

hands. Complaining of injuries and searching for the Santa who had thrown them off.

One by one, the elves regained their composure then threw themselves at Mike. He batted them off, hurling jingling bodies across the room. He puffed out his chest and bounced them off his padded stomach. He turned and twisted, slamming his enormous butt into them and sending them crashing to the floor.

Alex stood up. An elf looked up and screeched at her.

"Impostor!"

The elves turned to look at her, then back at Mike.

After a moment's collective hesitation, the crowd broke into two. Half of them rushed at her and the other half continued attacking Mike.

Mike pushed them off like a cat swatting at flies. They fell around him, a tangled mass of twisted limbs and high-pitched grumbling. Meanwhile, Alex had adopted the tactic of grabbing the hat from each elf that came at her and throwing it over the heads of the others. It confused the elves, who would then hurl themselves back into the crowd to find them. For some reason, those hats were important.

"Stop!"

The elves stopped moving. One, who had been jumping to to reach Alex's lofty height, stopped mid-leap, wild eyes staring at her, then dropped to the floor.

"Oof."

"Comrades, comrades! This is beneath you. We are elves, brothers. Sisters. And we are not only elves, but we are members of the Elf Liberation Organization. We are dignified, determined. Or at least some of us are."

The elves pulled back. Mike stood in their center, tensed. He was panting, his beard damp with sweat. The

Santa suit had slipped off his shoulder; beneath it was a red shirt, as vibrant as the jacket.

He stared at Horace. "What have you done with Santa?"

Horace approached Mike. He gestured towards one of the other red-suited elves. Three of the red suits closed in on Alex and grabbed her.

She looked around, searching for an escape route. But they were in the center of the room, surrounded by angry elves.

"Got it!"

An elf jumped up from the crowd, waving a hat. Its bell tinkled merrily.

"Shut up, Derek," said Horace.

Derek blushed. "Sorry, sir."

"Hmm." Horace looked at Mike. "I thought we'd got you all."

Mike stared back at him. He said nothing.

Alex struggled against the small hands holding her wrists and shoulders. There were six elves surrounding her. She was bigger than them, but not much, and if she did overpower these six, she'd have the other hundred to deal with.

"What's behind that door?" She pointed at the PRISON DO NOT ENTER door. The ribbon fluttered, glitter catching the light.

"None of your business," Horace replied. "Who are you, anyway? Have you been sent from Lapland?"

"Lapland? Yes. Of course I have."

The elf laughed, a high-pitched laugh that made Alex think of circuses. "You think you're clever, don't you? If you *are* from Lapland, we'd have been sent advance word."

"This is a spot check. An inspection. No warning.."

"Lapland don't do inspections."

"I'd watch what you say, Comrade," replied Alex. "I still have to decide what to put in my report."

"Your report?"

She thought over everything she'd heard them saying, before she'd been spotted.

"Yes. For HQ."

"Which HQ?"

She swallowed. "ELO HQ, of course. Christmas Island."

The elf paled. "You're from Elf Liberation Organization HQ?"

"Why do you think I'm so tall? They promote the big ones, you know."

Muttering ran through the elves. She spotted a few standing on tiptoe, measuring themselves against their colleagues. One, a clear three inches taller than the rest, beamed.

"She's right," said Mike. "And I'm incognito."

Horace turned to him. "Incognito?"

"In disguise, you idiot."

"I know what *incognito* means, Santa. It's just that you don't look it."

The elf drew closer to Mike. He put a hand out, his fingers stopping an inch from Mike's beard.

Mike stared at him, defiant. "Go on then."

Horace stretched his fingers out and touched the beard with their tips. It was as if he was expecting the soft white hair to burn him.

He visibly relaxed as his fingers delved further into Mike's beard. Mike watched, his nostrils flaring. Alex could only imagine how Mike felt about having this pumped-up elf shop steward poke around in his emabarassing facial hair.

"It's sticky," said the elf.

"Of course it is," said Alex. "Fake beards always are."

The elf turned to her. "Not in my experience."

"When you have to make them in a hurry, they are. And when the only manufacturing crew available to you is a team of elves who've stuffed so many sour candies into stockings that they're at risk of turning into lemons. Their fingers were sticky, see."

The elf fingered Mike's beard again. Mike pushed him away. He jerked his arms, freeing himself from the elves that had surrounded him.

"I suggest you let go of my colleague. She's a Lieutenant in the Christmas Island branch."

The redcoats around Alex gasped and pulled back. She brushed off her jacket, making a show of cleaning herself.

'Thank you," she said, casting a nervous glance at Mike. *What now?*

"That's better," said Mike. "Now, tell us your name and rank."

The chief elf swallowed, his Adam's apple bobbing up and down. He saluted. "Sergeant Horace Wimp, sir. At your service."

Mike smiled wryly. "Very good, Sergeant Wimp. Now show us your prisoners."

NINE

STOMACH

"OPEN THE DOOR, NORBERT," cried Horace. A green-suited elf scurried to the ribbon-festooned door and pushed it open. The ribbons fluttered to the floor.

The elves parted to make way. Horace held out an arm to wave Alex and Mike forward.

Alex shrugged at Mike then started walking. The elves shuffled and fidgeted around her as she passed between them. One of them muttered a *sorry*.

The doorway was dark.

"What's inside?" she asked.

Mike was behind her, peering over her head. His stomach pushed against her back. She grimaced and sucked herself in. Mike might be less objectionable now than when she'd first met him, but the feel of his rotund Santa belly made her flesh crawl like a river full of drowning ants.

Horace was behind them. He clicked his fingers and the doorway lit up. Behind it was a small space festooned with fairy lights.

"Odd kind of prison," Alex muttered.

"Worse than the one at the Hall of Justice," said Mike.

"Down the stairs," said Horace.

In the gloom beyond the fairy lights, the floor sank away. A shallow flight of stairs led downwards.

She turned back. This could be a trap.

"After you," she said to Horace.

He shook his head. "I couldn't possibly."

"I insist. Lead the way. Please."

He glanced at one of his red-suited companions then wove between Alex and Mike and under the fairy lights. His face glowed with the reflected light of a hundred multicolored bulbs, and his bell tinkled as he moved. Alex looked down to see that his shoes didn't have bells. A sign of status, or stealth mode?

The elves behind them pushed forward. Alex felt claustrophobic. If they hadn't believed her story, this was their moment to pounce. They could easily overwhelm the two of them and bundle them down the stairs to whatever prison it was they had at the bottom. With Mike's stomach the state it was in, they could roll him down.

Horace stepped forwards.

TEN

SANTAS

THE STAIRS LED into a vast underground chamber. The ceiling ahead of them was lit up by fairy lights, but beyond it was darkness. Alex could make out movement in the gloom, and hear soft, deep voices.

Horace reached the bottom of the stairs and stood to one side. He stared ahead of him, his face hard.

Alex stepped past him into the space, feeling the damp echoiness of it surround her. Mike followed her.

"What is this?" he breathed.

Horace straightened his back. He saluted.

"The prison, Sir."

Alex frowned. "Turn the lights on, then."

Horace clicked his fingers again. The glow from the fairy lights started to spread across the ceiling, flowing and shifting as it if were made of liquid. It took curling, looping trails, heading off at tangents then doubling back on itself until the whole room was a blaze of multi-colored light.

At the far end was what could only be described as a cage. Sure, it was a glittering cage festooned with tinsel and made of some kind of sparkling metal that seemed to have a life of its own. But it was a cage.

Inside it was a mass of red and white. Rotund bodies jostling against each other, breathing heavily. The acrid stench of sweat filled the space.

Alex stepped forwards. The Santas were having an argument.

"No, I tell you! It's December six, I tell you."

"Nonsense. Christmas Eve. The twenty-fifth. They decorate the tree and I bring gifts."

"That's wrong. On Christmas Eve, people exchange books. They go to bed to read them, and while they sleep I cover the globe on my sleigh and deliver the presents."

"Sleigh? What century do you live in? In my universe we use supersonic jets."

"Supersonic jets? That would wake the children."

"Well, drug them, then. Works for me."

"And what universe are you from?"

"Hell, don't ask me. I'm so spaced out I can't remember."

"Exactly."

"And what about the Christmas bear?"

"The Christmas armadillo, you mean."

"The Christmas bunny is what he's referring to."

"That's the Easter bunny."

"The Easter mongoose."

"The Easter pixie. Hides under toadstools and jumps out at children with miniature lampshades."

"What's Easter?"

"Don't ask. It's our rival. Where I come from, anyway."

"Will ye all shut up! Don't any of you know Hogmanay is by far the best festival?"

"Hogmanay's for losers."

"For boozers, you mean."

"Now don't knock Scotland's rich cultural heritage."

Alex stepped forward. She knew that voice.

"Dad?"

The Santas turned to her. A few of them weren't dressed in red at all, she noticed. At least twenty, thinner than their rotund rosy counterparts, wore green. One wore a skin-tight silver catsuit and a wooly hat. And another was dressed in nothing but a fur-trimmed red mankini.

She averted her eyes.

"Dad?" she called again. The Santas looked between each other, then back at her.

One of them, fortunately not the one in the mankini, stepped forward.

"Have you lost your Papa, my child?"

"No. How old do you think I am?"

"Twelve? What would you like for Christmas, kiddy?"

She frowned and looked over his shoulder.

"Duncan Strand, are you in there?"

There was jostling amongst the Santas. On of them muttered *Christmas Eve* and another snapped back *Three Kings' Day*.

Eventually the Santas in front parted and let one of their number through. He was a short, scrawny man with a beard that was so obviously fake a hamster could have worn it and made a more convincing Santa. Large black hooks held it to his face, curling over his ears, and his own two-day stubble poked out at the sides. His costume was equally pathetic: a red jacket with fur lining resembling glued-on cotton wool and a plastic belt with a buckle that looked like it would disintegrate at any moment.

"Alex?" he whispered.

Alex rushed forward. She put her arms through the sparkling bars of the cage. "Dad!"

She turned to the elves. "What the hell is my dad doing here?"

One of the red suits, not Horace, shrugged. "He's Santa."

"Look at him. Does he look like Santa to you?"

The elf blushed. "We have to work within fairly wide parameters here, you know. That Santa over there is wearing an obscene item of clothing, yet in his universe he's the real thing."

Alex resisted the admittedly weak temptation to look at the Santa in the mankini. She could sense the Santas behind her shuffling, maybe moving away from Mankini Santa. Or away from her dad.

"Well, I can tell you my dad's not the real thing. Let him go."

Horace put a hand on the other elf's arm. He offered Alex a thin smile. "I'm afraid we cannot do that."

"Why not? Surely you don't have a gripe with any old two-bit pound store fake Santa?"

"They all hold a little bit of the fabric that makes up the whole."

"The fabric that what? Don't talk bollocks."

"I'm not. When a person - or even a reindeer, or a cat, or a chipmunk - dons the Santa suit, a little bit of the magic transfers itself to them. If we can get all of them together it gives us great power."

"What sort of power?"

"I thought you said you were here from HQ?"

Alex blushed. "Yes."

"Well, you don't need me to tell you that then."

"It was another test."

Horace leaned towards her. "I'm not so sure about your tests."

He snapped his fingers. The room went dark. The Santas gasped.

Alex heard muffled cries behind her. She span round.

"Mike?"

Horace's voice came at her through the darkness. "We'll be taking this one too, thank you very much."

ELEVEN
CLICK

THE ROOM WAS QUIET. Alex put out her hands, groping in the darkness.

"Mike?"

No reply.

Alex stepped forwards, bracing herself for the thwack of an elf's face into her chest.

"Mike?"

"Alex?"

It wasn't Mike's voice; it was her dad's.

"Dad! Say my name again, so I can find you."

"Alex. I'm over here, lass."

She tstumbled towards the sound of his voice. "Again," she urged him.

"Right here. You're getting closer."

She took another tentative step, holding her arms out, feeling for his hands. Her palm hit something cold, and solid. The cage.

"I'm touching the cage, Dad. Which way are you?"

"I'm right here."

She felt something brush her wrist. She fumbled in the gloom. At last they were grasping each other's hands.

"It's good to see you, Dad."

"You too. Although maybe not like this, eh?"

"What happened to you?"

"He was snatched from the grotto," said a deep voice, English-sounding.

"Ignore him," said Duncan. "He's always interrupting."

"No, I'm not."

"See what I mean. Shut up, Santa, alright?"

"Same to you, Santa."

"Please, let me talk to my dad," Alex said. The English Santa muttered under his breath.

"What happened?" she asked.

"One minute I was sitting in the grotto. They made it out of discarded Tunnocks wrappers. Very impressive. Sparkly."

Alex could well imagine a grotto fabricated from the wrappers of Scotland's favorite chocolate cake (or biscuit, depending which side of the Tunnocks divide you were on).

"But how did you get here?"

"Hear me out, lass."

"Sorry."

"Like I said. One minute I was sitting there. Trying to stretch my legs after having an eighty-three-pound fifteen-year-old sitting on my lap and asking for an annual subscription to *Playboy* magazine. Cheeky wee bugger. Anyway. When I straightened up, I wasn't there anymore. I was here, surrounded by the most argumentative tribe of Santas I've ever seen in my life."

"Seen lots of tribes of Santas, have you Dad?"

"You know what I mean. So how did you get here?"

"Long story. But I'm here to take you home. You and all the other Santas."

"All of us?" The English Santa again.

Alex turned towards the patch of darkness where his voice had come from. "If I can, yes."

She knew she was here for the Macy's Santa, the Ur-Santa. But after what Horace had said, maybe each and every Santa here was a little fraction of the Ur-Santa. Even the one in the mankini.

"So how are you going to get us out then?" Another voice. Deeper, more Santa-like.

"I don't know." She considered. "Is Mike in there?"

"Who's Mike?"

"My colleague. The one they snatched just before the lights went out."

She looked upwards. It was as dark overhead as it was in front. She couldn't remember which way the staircase was.

She tried clicking her fingers. One fairy light came on, right above her head.

She stood on tiptoe to look at it. It was in a deeply tasteless shade of magenta.

She clicked her fingers again. Another light, green this time, fizzed and popped. She held her breath but it went out again.

She lowered her heels and looked towards the Santas. "Can you all give me a hand?"

"What with?" asked Duncan.

"Maybe if we all click our fingers, then a light will come on for each of us. More, if we're lucky."

"Worth a go." There was a pause. "Santas, did you hear her?"

"Hear what?"

"Pass the message on. In exactly ten seconds, I'll click my fingers. Then we all click, like a Mexican wave."

"If it's a Mexican wave, then you need to agree that we share the gift-giving job with the Wise Men."

"Whatever," said Duncan. "I share my gift-giving duties with a pimply twenty-three-year-old wearing a name badge. Wise Men have to be an improvement."

"Gracias."

Alex heard the message ripple through the crowd. Voices sprung up: deep, shrill, in as many accents as she had freckles on her nose. She recognized at least three languages, although there were more, one of which seemed to consist of guttural clicking sounds.

"Ready," said the Mexican Santa.

"Perfect," said Duncan. "You first, Alex."

She clicked her fingers. Duncan followed suit. The sound of his fingers snapping was followed by a ricochet of snaps.

She looked up at the magenta light, holding her breath. After what felt like an age, the light next to it (orange with a yellow center) flickered into life. Then the next, and the next, and the next. A wave of light rushed across the ceiling above the cage, in exactly the same way it had earlier.

She jumped for joy.

"Ow."

She'd hit her head on the low ceiling.

"You alright, lass?"

She rubbed her head. "I'm fine."

She wished she'd been wearing her elf hat; even its flimsy fabric would offer some protection. Then she tried to remember what had happened to it. To it, and the candy cane she'd slipped inside it for the jump. Sarita had told her to keep it safe. She'd have to be very hungry to resort to eating that.

The Santas glowed under the lights. They stood facing her, smiling. There was hope in their rotund faces.

Slumped on the floor next to Duncan. Leaning against the bars of the cage, was another Santa. She bent down. His eyes were closed, and he clutched a familiar elf hat.

"Mike?"

TWELVE

CHICKEN

"MIKE! MIKE, WAKE UP."

Duncan was level with Alex, crouched on the floor on the other side of the iridescent bars. He smiled at her.

"He your boyfriend, lass?"

Alex gave him a look. "How many times do I have to tell you, Dad?"

"I thought you might have expanded your tastes."

"It doesn't work like that."

"So does that mean you've got a girlfriend instead? Is she here with you?"

Alex blushed. "No."

"Not here? I'm sorry."

"No. No girlfriend."

"Ah. Maybe this fella would suffice while we're looking…"

"Dad. I don't go for guys. All right?"

Duncan raised his hands. "I just want you to be happy. To meet someone nice."

Alex thought of Sarita. An image of the MIU's material scientist in a close-fitting and skimpy Santa suit had been popping into her head unbidden. It did it again now.

She felt heat rise up her neck.

Duncan winked. "I won't say any more. But bring her home some time, yeah? Next visit?"

Alex lowered her eyes. She hadn't returned home in her two years in San Francisco, unable to bear the thought of entering the house where her mum had been murdered. Her dad, she knew, was disappointed, but chose not to say anything. He was a stoic Scotsman, despite all the whisky he drank, and not given to displays of emotion.

She murmured assent and he grunted.

"So. How are you going to get us out of here, now we've got illumination?"

Alex looked up at the ceiling then down at Mike. He was still unconscious.

She reached through the bars. Her elf hat was loose in his hand. She grabbed it.

"Fancy," said her dad.

She stuck out her tongue. "I didn't take it back to wear it."

"Why then?"

"This." She pulled the candy cane out of the hat's folds. It looked like a normal candy cane, red and white stripes and the customary hook.

She inspected it, feeling for buttons or pressure points. Nothing happened. She shook it.

"It's just a candy cane," her dad said.

She shook her head. "Sarita gave this to me. She wouldn't have done so without a reason."

"Who's Sarita?"

The blush spread further up her neck. "Our materials scientist."

"What's one of them?"

"Just another scientist." She remembered that as far as her dad was concerned, she was still working in the Physics faculty at the University of Berkeley.

"Oh. Pretty?"

She waved the candy cane in his face. "Shall we get back to trying to rescue you?"

"I was wondering when you'd say that."

A tall, rotund Santa with a full, genuine-looking beard was standing next to her dad. His suit was of a fine velvet and shimmered in the glow of the fairy lights.

"Which Santa are you?" she asked.

"The Macy's one."

"You're the ur-Santa? The real one?"

"In your universe, yes."

She gulped. "Cool."

"Did you enjoy the hobby horse I left for you when you were six? I got your letter."

Duncan cleared his throat. "She thinks that was me and her mum."

The ur-Santa laughed. "Don't be ridiculous." He cocked his head. "So, did you like it? My elves went to a lot of trouble."

"So it's your fault then," Alex said.

"You didn't like it?"

"Not the horse. I loved that."

It was true: she'd played with the thing until its paint wore off and its mane of once-thick hair was reduced to something you'd see on the back of a particularly ugly pig.

"I mean the elves," she said. "They're pissed off. You're working them into the ground."

"They love it," the ur-Santa replied. "They sing all day while they work."

"What do they sing?"

Santa shrugged. "No idea. It's in Russian."

"You don't speak Russian?"

"I dropped it when the Communists banned me. They wouldn't let the sleigh in, set up extra checkpoints on Christmas Eve."

Alex tried to imagine what was weirder: the Russians setting up anti-Santa checkpoints or the fact that she was standing in a cellar in a parallel universe arguing with the ur-Santa.

The Santas were squabbling again. Someone muttered *Elves, schmelves* and another shouted something about holly. She heard a punch land.

"Oi, you lot!" she yelled. They quietened.

"That's better," she said. This was the most unruly bunch of Santas she had ever seen. Worse even than when Rory McAdams and his mates had put on Santa hats and hung around Gretna's outlet village scaring the tourists.

"Does anyone here speak Russian?" she asked.

"Er, me." A hand went up.

"I need your help."

The Santas parted to let their Russian colleague through. He was thin, dressed in a long blue fur-trimmed coat. His beard was thick and flowing, almost down to his waist.

"Yes?"

"Can you translate something for me?" She turned to the ur-Santa. "Can you sing it?"

He looked at her like she'd asked him to swap outfits with the mankini Santa.

"Sing?" he asked.

"Well, hum it. Whatever. Just give us an idea of what the song might be."

The ur-Santa cleared his throat. He started warbling. Instead of the rich, deep-throated tones she'd been expecting, it was a sound that reminded her of a chicken being forced to sing *Jingle Bells*.

"I know that," said the Russian Santa.

The ur-Santa stopped singing. He looked sheepish.

"What is it?" asked Alex.

"It's a revolutionary song. From 1917. The Bolsheviks spread it."

Alex folded her arms across her chest. "See? Not happy. Not happy at all. They were planning a rebellion, and we're stuck in the middle of it."

THIRTEEN
SPLAT

ALEX SHOOK HER HEAD. He may be the ur-Santa, possessed of the ability to travel all the known worlds in one night, but when it came to people skills, he was clearly one elf short of a workshop.

"I'm getting you out of here," she said.

The ur-Santa pushed his shoulders back. He was huge, an imposing presence nothing like the Santas she'd encountered in shopping malls and school fairs in her childhood.

"No. The others first. You're my insurance policy."

"But I need to prepare for Christmas."

"You can't do that without your workforce."

The ur-Santa opened his mouth but then closed it again, chastened. Mike stirred.

"What's going on?"

"This eejit has created a Christmas revolution," Alex replied.

"Which eejit?"

She pointed at the ur-Santa. He lifted his chest even higher, refusing to be cowed by a short ginger Scotswoman.

She sniffed. "Let's use this thing."

She twisted the candy cane. It felt soft and smooth in her hand, and had lost the customary stickiness.

Nothing happened.

"D'you think that'll do something?" Mike asked. He was pulling up to his feet now, rubbing his forehead. A swelling the size of a satsuma was forming.

"Sarita gave it to us for a reason." She stroked it, then twisted it again. She pulled it at both ends. Nothing happened.

She frowned at it.

"It's not an ordinary candy cane," she said. "It can't be."

"Only one way to find out," said Mike.

He was right. She closed her eyes and brought it to her lips. She closed her teeth over it. It was hard. Her dentist would rub his hands with glee if he could see this.

She squeezed her eyes shut and bit.

There was a *splat* sound. She opened her eyes. The Santas were looking around, muttering.

"Again!" one of them cried.

She took another bite. Another noise, a *whoosh* this time. A ripple of applause came from the crowd of Santas.

She crunched into the cane again and again, taking tiny nibbles. With every bite, there was another sound. Some were accompanied by a flash of sparkly light from deep within the crowd.

The crowd was thinning. With each bite, a Santa disappeared. She sped up, crunching through the candy cane until only her dad and the ur-Santa were left.

She hesitated. Her dad was smiling at her, his eyes wet. She wondered if he'd remember this.

The ur-Santa's bushy brows were knotted, like two

longhaired white cats fighting over a morsel of catnip. She glared at him.

She bit. Her dad gasped then disappeared into thin air. There was a pink flash of light and a single note that sounded suspiciously like it had been played on bagpipes.

There was only a morsel of the candy cane left. One bite.

The ur-Santa gestured at it. "Go on."

"No. You need to fix this."

"You certainly do."

They turned to see a throng of elves swarming into the cellar behind them. They were advancing quietly, the only sound the faint jangling of the bells on their shoes and hats.

"Bite it. Now," the ur-Santa said.

She turned to him. "You want to be a coward? Is that what all those children think of you?"

His eyebrows started fighting again. He twisted his mouth at her.

She felt a small hand on her arm, and another on her leg. She pulled away but more hands had landed on her, tugging her back and forth.

Mike had sunk into the crowd of elves, shouting at them from deep within the throng. The fairy lights were dimming and her vision shrank to a small patch of light containing just her, Horace and the ur-Santa.

"Kosh her."

Horace shifted to let one of his colleagues through. He was holding a rubber mallet.

"No! I can help!" she cried.

The mallet hit her face and the world went black.

FOURTEEN
SANTA BABY

ALEX WOKE to find herself in a low-ceilinged room. She sat up, rubbing her head.

Mike was next to her, his legs chained to the wall with something that looked like tinsel but was as strong as steel. Beyond him, the ur-Santa filled half of the room, his head brushing the ceiling.

"What happened?" she asked. "Are you ok?"

"I'm fine," said the ur-Santa.

"I didn't mean you." She reached out to Mike. He was pale, and the exposed skin where the tinsel-steel encircled his leg was raw.

She stood up, then regretted it when she hit the ceiling. She collapsed to the floor. Stars swam in front of her eyes, twirling and sparkling red and green.

Behind the ur-Santa was a small door. She crawled towards it, shoving his fat legs out of the way. He grunted at her.

She hammered on the door.

"Let us out! We can help you!"

A hatch in the door slid open and a rosy-cheeked face appeared. "Be quiet, prisoner. We don't need you."

"But you do. I know what's happening. I'm on your side."

"You're protecting those two Santas. Including the big guy."

"He isn't a big guy."

"Look at him."

"He may be imposing, but inside he's smaller than any of you. He's treated you like crap, hasn't he? Working all the hours, three hundred and sixty four days a year?"

The elf frowned. "If you think you're going to get round us by pretending to—"

"I'm not pretending anything. I can see what he's been doing. I know about your songs."

"How?"

"There was a Russian Santa in that cellar."

Another face appeared at the hatch: Horace.

"Hey, Horace," Alex said.

"Don't *Hey Horace* me. You're one of them. We're still deciding what to do with you."

"Let me out. Let me talk to you. Me and my colleague."

"You freed the Santas. With that cane of yours."

"Not the ur-Santa. He wanted me to send him off, but I refused."

The hatch closed. She heard muttering. It increased in pitch, turning into angry shouts.

It opened again. She pasted on a smile. Mike was behind her now, having climbed over the ur-Santa's legs. The ur-Santa was singing *Santa Baby* to himself.

"No," said Horace.

"You're making a mistake."

"We don't believe you. You can stay there till Boxing Day."

"You can't do that."

The hatch slammed shut.

Alex slumped back. She was stuck in a tiny room in a parallel universe with a Santa who'd proved to be nothing like the myths she'd believed and another who was recovering from a blow to the head. She had no idea where thecae had sent the other Santas. She could only hope her dad was safe.

And Christmas only knew where Rudolph had got to.

She pulled the remains of the candy cane from inside her elf outfit. Luckily it was too small for the elves to have spotted it.

She looked at the ur-Santa.

"You don't deserve this, you know," she told him.

She popped the candy into her mouth and bit down.

There was a pop and a puff of smoke.

Mike had disappeared. She was alone with the ur-Santa. And all the candy had gone.

FIFTEEN
FAT CAT

HE LOOKED down at her empty hand. "You were supposed to get me out of here."

"I'm supposed to fix this situation. If you don't make nice with those elves, Christmas won't be happening. You need to negotiate with them."

"Negotiate? I'm Santa. The real thing. Saint Nick. Father Christmas. Sinterklaas. Kris Kringle. I don't negotiate with anyone."

"Things change."

He shook his head. "I don't."

"Yes, you do."

"No, I don't."

He spread his legs wide, filling the space. She shifted away from him then thought better of it and pushed back.

"Tell me," she said. "How do you get down all those chimneys?"

"You should know that."

"You're right. It's quantum entanglement. Means you can be in two places at once, no matter how distant.

Multiply it out and you can be everywhere in the multiverse at the same time."

"That hobby horse was wasted on you."

"So why can't you apply that to the workshop?"

"The workshop isn't my responsibility. It's the elves'"

"But you oversee things."

"Not since the Christmas Eve uprising of 1913."

"The what?"

"They rebelled. Told me they wouldn't do what I said anymore. Took over management themselves." He stroked his beard. "I have to admit, they turned out to be rather good at it. And it means I can put my feet up between Christmas Eves."

"You really are a fat cat, aren't you?"

He stopped stroking. "Don't compare me to one of those ghastly creatures."

"You know what I mean. Sitting on your massive behind, taking all the credit for the work the elves do. There are plenty like you on my Earth."

"I don't know what you're talking about. Christmas would be nothing without me."

"Hmmpf."

He went back to stroking his beard. She watched him, the germ of an idea growing. *Fat cat...*

She hammered on the door.

"Elves!" she shouted. "I know how to solve all your problems. I just need a box!"

SIXTEEN
BOX

THE HATCH OPENED. It was a new elf, dressed in a purple jacket and yellow tights.

"Nice outfit," she said. "Sarita would approve."

"Flattery won't get you anywhere."

"Sorry. Look, I know how to fix this. I just need a cardboard box."

"A cardboard box?"

"Yes. An empty one."

"I don't believe you."

"I promise you, this is for real."

"You're just going to get in it and disappear."

"How would I do that?"

A shrug. "You're with him. You're going to play a trick on us."

Horace shoved the purple and yellow elf to one side.

"What are you trying to get past Violet here?"

"I need an empty cardboard box. I can use it to solve your problem. Reduce your workload."

"How is a cardboard box going to reduce our workload? Do you know the hours he makes us work?"

"I do. And I think it's wrong. But I can help."

"Why should I believe you?"

"Just let me try. A box, please?"

He rubbed his nose. It glowed at the tip.

"Alright then. But out here, with us watching. And *he* stays in there."

The hatch slammed shut.

Alex stared at it, her breath shallow. The ur-Santa was breathing down her neck. She pushed him away.

"You heard them."

He muttered and drew back. "You'd better get us out of here."

"I will," she said. "And you'll start treating those elves with some respect. You don't want to put Christmas at risk again, do you?"

He wrinkled his nose.

There was the sound of a lock being slid open. Then another, and another. At last the door opened a crack. A small purple arm came through and grabbed Alex. Violet pulled her through the door, her feet skittering on the wooden floor.

She stumbled out, struggling to stay upright. The door slammed shut behind her.

She leaned against it, staring at the elves. Dozens of them surrounded her, their small beady eyes menacing.

They were in a workshop. Long tables lined the walls, rolls of wrapping paper strewn on them and interspersed with toys. Bikes, toy ponies, LEGO Batmen. A Barbie stared at her, its blue glare accusing.

Horace wove through the crowd. He held a brown cardboard box at arm's length.

"Here you are. Prove yourself."

"Thank you."

She took the box and held it in front of her. Her idea

had seemed so sensible when she was talking to the ur-Santa, so scientifically logical. But now she was standing in a room full of angry legs armed with nothing but a cardboard box.

She opened the box's lid. It was empty. She stared into it, remembering what the ur-Santa had told her about quantum entanglement.

She looked back at the elves. They were looking from her to the box. She could sense them tapping their feet.

"I need you all to look away," she said.

Horace shook his head. "You think we're stupid?"

"It doesn't work unless you're not observing it. Don't you see? That's how Santa does it. It's why only children who are asleep get a visit. Because *they can't observe him.*"

"If we look away, you'll escape."

"My only way out is back into that room. And you know I can't get out of there, or you wouldn't have shut me in in the first place."

Horace stopped rubbing his nose.

"And if I try to run through you, you'll feel me. Even with your eyes closed."

Horace sniffed. He pulled at his nose.

"Alright then. But only for a few seconds."

"Perfect. You can count to five, and keep your eyes closed only for that long."

Horace raised a hand. The buzz that had been passing through the elves stopped.

"Did you hear that, comrades? On my mark, we're all to close our eyes for the count of five."

"Why?" came a voice at the back of the crowd.

"Because the physics won't work if we're watching."

Alex nodded at Horace. He understood.

He narrowed his eyes at her. "This had better not be a trick."

"It isn't."

I hope. She closed the lid of the box.

Horace raised his hand higher. "Now!"

The elves closed their eyes. Alex scanned them, checking that all eyes were closed.

"One," said Horace.

There was a cough from the center of the crowd. Alex saw an elf open his eyes. She frowned at him and he closed them again.

"Two!"

She took a deep breath. She looked down at the box, feeling its weight in her hands. It was flimsy. She hoped they used sturdier boxes on Christmas Eve.

"Three!"

Alex looked up at the ceiling. Her heart was pounding. Behind her, she could hear the ur-Santa. He was singing *Santa Baby* again.

She frowned.

"Four!"

The elves all had their eyes closed. Their chests rose and fell as one. It was as if they were in a trance.

She squeezed her eyes shut.

"Five!"

She felt the box shift in her hands. It was heavy. It was moving.

She opened her eyes. The elves were staring at her. She gripped the box tightly, worried it would slip from her hands.

Her heart thudding against her ribcage, she prized the box open. If she was right, they would change Christmas forever. But what sort of gift would be in there? And why was it moving?

She opened the lid fully. A head popped out. A familiar head. She stared into its eyes.

"Miaow?"

"SHRODINGER!"

Alex scooped the cat out of the box and gave him a hug.

"How did you get here, boy?"

"Miaow."

"Yes, I know. The magic of being a quantum cat. Well done. But you were supposed to be a present."

"Miaow."

"You'd make the perfect present. I know. But I don't think you're what the elves need."

"What's going on?" Horace glared at Alex's fat ginger cat, the tip of his nose glowing red.

"This is Shroedinger. He's a quantum cat. Likes boxes."

"I can see that. How does he solve our problems? We can't give every child a cat."

"I'm sure they'd love it if you did."

"Their parents wouldn't. Not to mention the bird population."

"Miaow."

"Sorry, Shrew," said Alex. "I'm sure he didn't mean to insult you."

"Miaow."

There was a thump at the door behind her. The ur-Santa was getting impatient.

She opened the hatch. "I'm getting there."

"It doesn't sound like it. I can't put cats in all the stockings, you know."

"No."

Alex turned back to the elves.

"You need to let him out."

"No way."

"The physics will only work with the combination of Santa and the box. And it has to be the right kind of box."

"All you've given us so far is a cat."

"Miaow."

"Shush," Alex told Shroedinger. "You need to go home."

"Miaow."

Shrodinger wasn't going anywhere. She held him under her arm, not an easy feat given the number of mince pies he'd been stealing from the kitchen cupboard when she wasn't looking. There were many advantages to being a quantum cat.

"OK," she said. "Let me try one more time. I need three things."

"Three? I thought you just needed the box?" said Horace.

"That wasn't enough. I need a Christmassy box, not a plain one. And a letter. A child's letter to Santa. And I need Santa to be holding the box. Or at least touching it."

"What else will you be wanting, the reindeer?"

"I'll do it in there." She gestured towards the room

where Santa was imprisoned. "You don't have to let him out."

"Very well."

Horace opened the door, wagging a finger at Santa to make sure he didn't budge. He pushed Alex back in. Shroedinger struggled under here arm but she managed to hang onto him, finally letting go when the door had been closed.

"Miaow."

"Who's this?" asked Santa.

"Shroedinger. He's my cat. He has quantum powers."

Santa ran a large hand down Shrodinger's back. Shrodinger arched towards him, purring.

"He likes me."

"You don't deserve him."

"So what's all this about me holding a box?"

"You'll see."

The hatch opened. A brightly-wrapped box was pushed through, and an envelope.

Alex opened it and read the letter inside. "This'll do."

The purple and yellow elf, Violet, was peering through the hatch.

"Letters is my job," she said. "That's one of my favorites. I get fed up of the kids who ask for ponies, or kittens, or world peace."

"Thank you. I'll let you have it back as soon as we're done. But I need you to close that hatch."

She sniffed and closed it.

Alex turned to the ur-Santa. "Now I need you to hold these. Close your eyes."

The ur-Santa took the box and the letter. He rolled the letter up loosely, closed the box and placed the letter on its lid. Then he held them in his outstretched hands. HIs pudgy fingers made the box look tiny.

"I'll count to three, then we both close our eyes," said Alex.

"Go on."

"One, two—"

"Three!" shouted the ur-Santa.

Alex closed her eyes. She put her hand over Shrodinger's face. He struggled against her but she held on tight.

There was a sound. A voice.

Alex tore the box open. There was a doll inside, with large yellow eyes.

"Are you my mummy?" it said.

"Takes all sorts," said the ur-Santa.

She banged on the door. "It worked! Let us out."

The hatch opened again: Horace. "Show me."

She held up the box, and the doll.

"I love you," the doll said.

"You didn't smuggle that in?"

"It appeared in the box. Just like Shroedinger here in his box."

Horace narrowed his eyes at her.

"Let us out," she said. "He can replicate it."

"Me?" said the ur-Santa. "Just how many presents do you want me to materialize?"

"Don't worry," she said. "It's like the way you travel around the world. As long as the boxes are touching, you can do as many as you want at a time. The elves just have to assemble the boxes and the letters."

"I can do that!" came Violet's voice.

"What if they don't have letters?" asked Horace.

"You'll work something out," said Alex. "Maybe they'll duplicate from the ones with letters. Maybe you'll hack into their computer cookies."

"Go on," said Violet. "The letters have the power. Let's do it!"

The door opened. Alex motioned for the ur-Santa to pass. He shuffled out on his hands and knees. He was greeted by a hard silence from the elves.

"How do we know he'll do it?" one of them asked.

"If he doesn't, Christmas won't happen," said Alex. "You don't want that, do you Santa?"

"I suppose not."

"That's it then. Violet, get some more letters. Make a pile of boxes."

The elves dashed around the room, jostling each other. Violet ran outside and returned with a bulging sack full of letters. Her comrades piled gift-wrapped boxes on the tables and she tossed the letters into them.

"Right. Let's all close our eyes," said Alex. "One, two, three—now!"

She scrunched her eyes shut. The room went quiet. Then there was a sound, a tiny clapping sound. It was followed by the beep of an electric toy. Then more beeping, and some whirring.

She opened her eyes. The beeping and whirring had been joined by louder, more worrying sounds. Miaowing. Barking. The squeak of hamsters. And a pony braying. It tore its way out of a box, shaking its pink mane.

Violet shrugged. "We were lucky. Normally more of them ask for ponies."

Shroedinger leaped out of Alex's arms and into the melee. Torn-up wrapping paper lay in piles on the floor, a menagerie of creatures tearing through it. Dogs ran after cats, cats ran after mice, and hamsters hid in the gaps between floorboards. The pony looked at it all dismissively then started chewing the paper.

"This isn't what we wanted," said Horace.

"Sorry," said Alex.

"It's alright," said the ur-Santa. "I can temper it."

"Temper it?"

"While you all had your eyes shut, I was working hard. Imagining the children getting their perfect gift. I can amend my thought processes, shut out any thoughts of live creatures."

Shroedinger screeched and jumped into Alex's arms.

"Not you, Shrew," said the ur-Santa, bending to tickle between his ears. He narrowed his eyes at the man. Alex wondered if they understood each other.

"You'll let me go, then," she said to Horace. "And tell me where Mike is."

"I can do the first," he said. "But I have no idea where your partner is. That's all on you."

EIGHTEEN

NOSE

ALEX STUMBLED THROUGH THE SNOW. The elves had given her a cat basket for Shroedinger and she clutched it to her chest, ignoring his annoyed miaows.

"Its all your fault for refusing to go into another box," she told him.

"Miaow."

"Yes I know it had a picture of dog food on it, but still."

"Miaow."

She shook her head and trudged forwards. The elves had let her go but were unable to help her get home. She'd come here using Hive technology and she'd have to go back the same way.

Which meant finding Rudolph.

She whistled.

"Rudolph!" she called. It was getting dark, and the paper-snow-covered trees glowed in the dusk.

He could be anywhere.

She headed down the hill. She thought of following her footsteps from earlier but there were none; either because more snow had fallen, or more likely because paper snow didn't form footsteps.

She looked towards the white Bay, trying to remember which way the Hall of Justice was from Mount Davidson. Normally she'd have the map of the streetlights to guide her, but here the fairy lights fell away in straight lines, fanning out from the cabin.

She came to the bottom of the hill. Trees loomed at her from all sides. The sky had darkened, and was the color of a whale instead of a porpoise.

They arrived in a clearing. She heard something up ahead.

"Miaow."

"Shush, Shrew. It's all right."

She pushed through the trees.

Rudolph was ahead of them, nibbling at a shrub that sat in the centre of an almost perfectly circular clearing.

She ran towards him, ignoring Shroedinger's hisses.

"Rudolph! Good boy!"

He looked up at her, then moved away.

She had Rudolph, but where was Mike? She'd never find him in the dark.

"Bon garçon!" she cried. "Viens!"

He stopped moving. He eyed her, then the hissing moggy in her arms.

He sneezed, sending globules of red and green reindeer snot her way. His nose began to glow.

"You've got a cold, boy."

He rolled his upper lip back, baring large teeth.

"Le nez," she said, pointing at her own nose.

He sniffled and plodded towards her. As she stroked his nose, a shape appeared beside him. She bent down to puck it up. It was a parcel, with a perfect green bow. The bitbox.

She shook it. Mike didn't like her using the bitbox and

she had no idea how this one worked. She tugged at the ribbon.

"Hello?"

She stopped tugging. "Madge?"

"Alex. You're breaking up."

She tugged a little more. Madge's glowing face appeared in the side of the gift.

"Have you heard from Mike?" Alex asked.

"He's here. Appeared on my desk out of nowhere. Made such a mess, he did. Where are you?"

"I'm in San TaClaus. I've got Rudolph."

"What about Santa? He disappeared from the morgue."

"He's going to be fine. The others, are they—"

"They're all back in their grottos. As far as we know, anyway."

"I can't find the Spinner."

"That's easy. Rudolph will show you."

"He will?"

She eyed Rudolph. He was sneezing into the fake snow, sending gusts of paper flying.

"Rudolph, find the Spinner."

He looked up at her.

"I don't know what it is in French, you silly reindeer. Le Spinner."

Rudolph snorted. An object appeared next to him. It was smooth, and white, and cylindrical. A door swish-thunked open in its side.

She grabbed Rudolph's reins and pulled him in with her and Shrodinger.

NINETEEN

DREAM

ALEX CLATTERED INTO HER APARTMENT, Shrödinger still in the box the elves had given her. She opened it and let him jump out. She opened the window a crack, watching him slide out onto the balcony. He stopped to miaow at a pigeon that sat on the railings.

She slumped onto the sofa. Mike had been waiting for her in the MIU when she got back. Without Rudolph, Madge and Nemesis had been unable to send him back to San TaClaus, and he'd been suffering from concussion anyway.

Not to mention a severe case of embarrassment at the state of his beard. It was long and wispy, and trailed down to the floor. By the time Alex had arrived, Madge had plaited it. For the sake of practicality.

Alex pulled her mobile from her pocket. She was in her jeans and jacket again, the elf suit back in Sarita's wardrobe.

"Gretna three five nine two."

"Dad!"

"Alex?"

"Dad, are you alright? Did you get back safe?"

"What? What are you on about, lass?"

"You were in San TaClaus. With me. The candy cane sent you back."

"Santa Claus? Candy cane? What are you on about?"

She smiled. It was probably for the best.

"Sorry, Dad. I've been out partying. Too much American beer."

"Eww. Gnat's piss, all of it. Drink some whisky, lass."

"Yes Dad."

"Anyway, it's four in the afternoon. And it's Christmas Eve. Why are you calling me now?"

"Nothing, dad. Nothing. Did you do your Santa shift today?"

"No. Funny, it was. They cancelled it. Said the grotto had gone missing."

"Oh."

"Anyway, they've asked me to do a special Christmas Eve stint this evening. For late shoppers."

"Be careful, Dad."

"What of? Kids widdling on my lap? Teenagers pulling at my beard?"

"Nothing, Dad. Just be careful. I'll call you tomorrow."

"Right y'are. Speak to you in the morning. Merry Christmas."

"Merry Christmas."

"And don't forget."

"Don't forget what?"

"That lassie of yours. The materials scientist, you said."

Alex stiffened. "She's not my lassie."

"Whatever. Bring her home next Christmas, eh? I'd like to meet her."

JOIN THE MIU

Have you got what it takes to be a Multiverse Investigator?

Join us now and receive each new Multiverse Investigations story for FREE as it's published.

Join now at multiverse-investigations.com/join.

Catawampus Press

catawampus-press.com